LIGHTNING BOLT BOOKS™

Meet a Baby Horse

Buffy Silverman

Lerner Publications • Minneapolis

Lerner Publications Company
A division of Lerner Publishing Group, Inc.
241 First Avenue North
Minneapolis, MN 55401 USA

For reading levels and more information, look up this title at www.lernerbooks.com.

Library of Congress Cataloging-in-Publication Data

Names: Silverman, Buffy, author.
Title: Meet a baby horse / Buffy Silverman.
Description: Minneapolis: Lerner Publications, [2016] | Series: Lightning bolt books. Baby farm
    animals | Audience: Ages 5–8. | Audience: K to grade 3. | Includes bibliographical references and
    index.
Identifiers: LCCN 2015037234| ISBN 9781512408010 (lb : alk. paper) | ISBN 9781512412383
    (pb : alk. paper) | ISBN 9781512410273 (eb pdf)
Subjects: LCSH: Foals—Juvenile literature. | Horses—Juvenile literature.
Classification: LCC SF302 .S5625 2016 | DDC 636.1/07—dc23

LC record available at http://lccn.loc.gov/2015037234

Manufactured in the United States of America
1 – BP – 7/15/16

Table of Contents

Long Legs

A newborn horse lies in a field and whinnies. Its mother nuzzles and licks it. She cleans the baby horse.

The mother nudges her baby. The foal struggles to stand on its long legs.

A baby horse is called a foal.

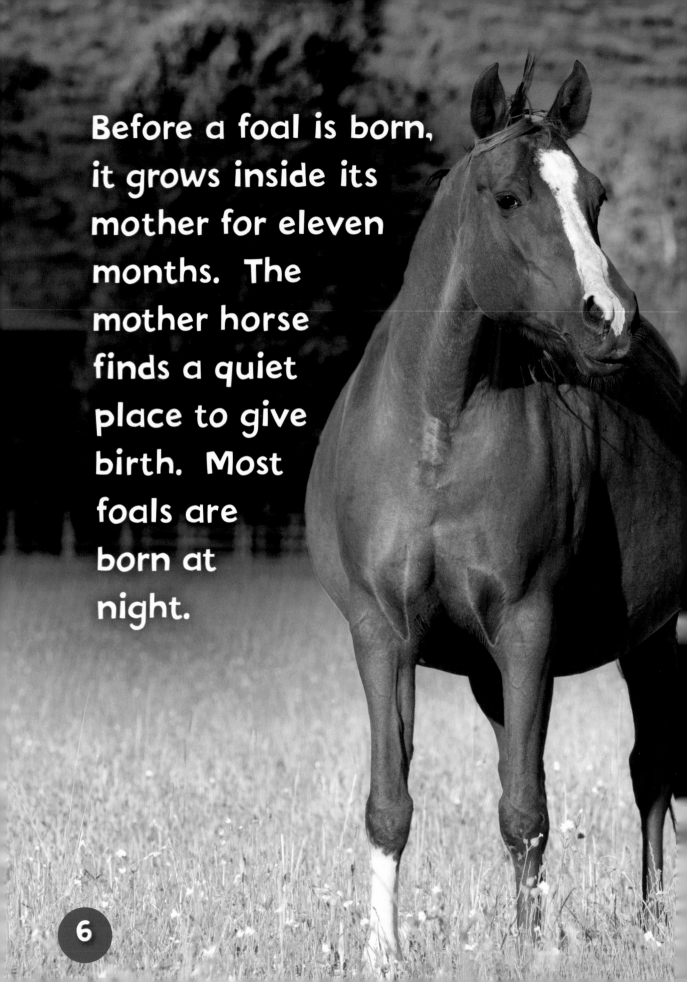

Before a foal is born, it grows inside its mother for eleven months. The mother horse finds a quiet place to give birth. Most foals are born at night.

This foal is one hour old. It stands and reaches its head under its mother. The foal sniffs. Soon it finds her teat and drinks milk.

The mother's milk has
extra nutrients that keep
the baby horse healthy.
The mother gets to know
her baby while it drinks.

She sniffs her foal. She learns to recognize the foal by smell and sight. She listens to the foal's snorts and neighs.

This foal is getting used to its long legs.

A foal's head and body are much smaller than those of an adult horse. But its legs are almost as long as an adult's legs. The foal's first steps are wobbly.

A newborn foal weighs about 100 pounds (45 kilograms), as much as two seven-year-old children. A mother horse usually weighs ten times as much as her foal. That's as heavy as twenty seven-year-olds!

Following Mom

A foal trots a few hours after it is born. The foal does not yet recognize its mother. It follows any animal that moves. It would follow a person too.

On its first day, a foal learns how its mother smells and looks. The baby horse listens when she nickers. Its long legs help the foal keep up with its mom. The foal stays close.

The foal does not leave its
mother for its first month.
It nurses many times a day.

The baby horse is tired. It lies down to nap. The mother horse keeps her foal safe.

Foals spend most of their time nursing and napping.

When a foal wakes up,
it runs around its mom.
It jumps and kicks its
feet. It plays by itself.

One-month-old foals start
to play with other foals.
They run and kick. They
pretend to fight. They
scratch one another's
backs with their teeth.

Growing, Growing, Growing

Young foals nurse often.
They grow quickly. Their
weight doubles in four weeks.

This foal has started eating hay.

When a foal is between one and three weeks old, it starts to nibble hay. It eats hay and oats.

A foal has a short neck.
That makes it hard for the
foal's head to reach the
ground. It spreads its front
legs. Then its head can get
low enough to chew grass.

A two-month-old foal wanders away from its mom. It spends more time eating on its own. It plays with other foals until it is tired. Then it lies down to sleep.

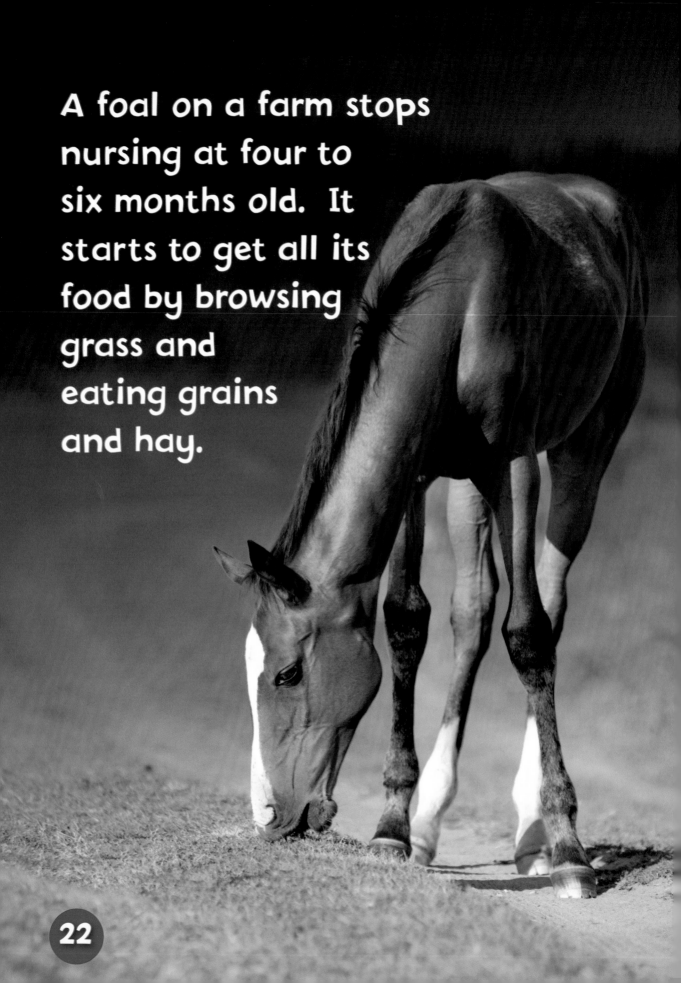

A foal on a farm stops nursing at four to six months old. It starts to get all its food by browsing grass and eating grains and hay.

Ready to Work

A one-year-old horse is steady on its legs. It gallops and plays with other yearlings.

A one-year-old horse is called a yearling.

23

The yearling spends less time napping and lying down than foals do. Yearlings can sleep while standing up.

A young horse holds its head out and clacks its teeth. That shows that it will obey other horses in a herd. It learns to obey people too.

A two-year-old horse can wear a saddle. It grows stronger and stronger. Soon it will be able to carry a rider or pull a cart.

This four-year-old horse is fully grown. Soon she will have a foal of her own!

A horse may live for thirty years or more.

Why People Raise Horses

Most horses live on farms. Some horses are raised for riding. Others are raised for racing. Some horses learn to compete in shows. Horses work on some farms by pulling wagons and plows. Sometimes they haul logs. Ranchers ride horses when they move cattle. Some horses pull wagons or sleighs for hayrides.

Fun Facts

- An adult female horse is called a mare. An adult male horse is called a stallion.

- People have used horses for at least five thousand years. Horses pulled chariots across Europe and Asia four thousand years ago. Today almost all horses are owned by people.

- People change horses' traits by choosing which horses to breed. A tall horse might be bred with another tall horse. Usually that will make a tall baby horse.

- There are more than two hundred kinds of horses. Some can race across fields. Others pull heavy loads. Some horses are as big as a moose. Some are as small as dogs.

Glossary

browse: to feed on grass and other plants

foal: a horse that is less than one year old

gallop: to run very fast

nicker: a soft noise made by a horse

nurse: to drink milk from a mother's body

nutrient: a substance in food that an animal needs to grow and stay healthy

saddle: a seat placed on the back of a horse for a rider

teat: the part of a mother's body through which milk flows

trot: a slow run

whinny: a neighing sound, often made by a horse that is looking for another horse

yearling: a horse that is between twelve and twenty-four months old

Further Reading

All about Horses
http://www.godolphinkids.co.uk/all
-about-horses

American Museum of Natural History: Horse
http://www.amnh.org/exhibitions/horse

Life Cycle of a Horse
http://www.pklifescience.com/article/504/life
-cycle-of-a-horselogin?username=thealberta&pass
word=library

Nelson, Robin. *From Foal to Horse*. Minneapolis:
Lerner Publications, 2012.

Silverman, Buffy. *Can You Tell a Horse from a Pony?* Minneapolis: Lerner Publications, 2012.

Index

Photo Acknowledgments

The images in this book are used with the permission of: © iStockphoto.com/ acceptfoto, p. 2; © Tierfotoagentur/Alamy, pp. 4, 5, 9; © iStockphoto.com/DFeinman, p. 6; © petcharaPJ/Thinkstock, p. 7; © iStockphoto.com/tolgaildun, p. 8; © Alex Sharp/ Photographer's Choice/Getty Images, p. 10; © iStockphoto.com/elrphoto, p. 11; © iStockphoto.com/Zuzule, pp. 12, 16; © iStockphoto.com/tamaw, p. 13; © iStockphoto. com/KentWeakley, p. 14; © iStockphoto.com/albanwr, p. 15; © Animals Animals/ SuperStock, p. 17; © iStockphoto.com/schnuddel, p. 18; © Steen Wackerhausen/ Thinkstock, p. 19; © iStockphoto.com/Ansaharju, p. 20; © iStockphoto.com/volgariver, p. 21; © iStockphoto.com/mari_art, p. 22; © iStockphoto.com/Zelenenka, p. 23; © iStockphoto.com/Northlife, p. 24; © TiggyMorse/iStock/Thinkstock, p. 25; © iStockphoto.com/virgonira, p. 26; © iStockphoto.com/DHuss, p. 27; © iStockphoto. com/winhorse, p. 28; © Gay Bumgarner/Alamy, p. 30.

Front cover: © mariait/Shutterstock.com.

Main body text set in Johann Light 30/36.